Walt Disney's
Winnie the Pooh
and the Missing Bullhorn

Written by Michael Teitelbaum
Illustrated by Russell Schroeder and Don Williams

A GOLDEN BOOK • NEW YORK
Western Publishing Company, Inc., Racine, Wisconsin 53404

                                                                  MCMXCII

Winnie the Pooh had just finished his pre-breakfast smackerel of honey. "I think I'll go for a walk before eating my real breakfast," said Pooh. And he decided to stroll over to visit Christopher Robin.

Christopher Robin was in his backyard playing with a bullhorn that he had found.

"Hello, out there!" Christopher Robin said into the bullhorn. His voice boomed loudly out the other end of the horn.

"This bullhorn makes my voice much louder," thought Christopher Robin. "If I talk through it I can be heard all over the Hundred-Acre Wood."

"Good morning, Christopher Robin!" Pooh said with a smile. "What do you have there?"

"This is a bullhorn," said Christopher Robin, handing it to Pooh. Just then, Christopher Robin's mother called him in to clean up his room. "I've got to go, Pooh. Keep the bullhorn if you like."

Pooh stood there holding the bullhorn and thinking, "This doesn't look like any horn I've ever seen on a bull! Besides, bullhorns usually come attached to bulls. This is very puzzling."

Pooh decided to ask his friends about the strange object. He took the bullhorn and went to find Piglet. Pooh soon came upon Piglet and Tigger. Tigger was trying to teach Piglet how to bounce like a Tigger.

"Oh, but, Tigger," said Piglet nervously, "do you think a small animal like myself could ever learn to bounce like a tigger?"

"Indisputadubitably!" answered Tigger.

"Oh," said Piglet. "Does that mean yes?"

"Excuse me, Piglet, Tigger," interrupted Pooh, who had been standing there quietly for a few minutes.

"Why, good morning, Pooh!" said Piglet.

"Watcha got there, buddy boy?" asked Tigger when he noticed the bullhorn in Pooh's hand.

"Christopher Robin called it a bullhorn," explained Pooh, "but I'm wondering why it was in his backyard and not on a bull's head, where it belongs."

"I think I know, Pooh," said Piglet. "I remember seeing a bull with only one horn, out in the Rolling Pasture. I heard that he lost his other horn in a fight with another bull, and now he is very mean and dangerous!"

This story frightened Pooh, but the more he thought about it, the more he felt that he had to return the bullhorn to its rightful owner. "Returning the horn to the bull," thought Pooh, "would be the polite thing to do. If I lost my honey, I would want someone to return it to me. Besides, when the bull sees the good deed I'm doing, he couldn't possibly be angry with me. Why, he might even invite me in for some honey! That is, if bulls eat honey."

So off Pooh went to the Rolling Pasture, to find the bull with the missing horn.

Meanwhile, Piglet was worried about Pooh's meeting with the bull. "I think we should follow him, Tigger," said Piglet, "in case he needs some rescuing!"

"No sweat, little buddy," began Tigger. "Rescuing is what tiggers do best!" The two friends followed Pooh to the Rolling Pasture.

When Pooh arrived at the Rolling Pasture, he saw some
farms, some houses, and a picnic area. Right next to the
picnic area, in a fenced-off pen, stood the bull with the
missing horn. The huge creature grunted and snorted as he
pawed the ground with his hoof.

"Hello, Mister Bull with the missing horn," shouted Pooh. "Look what I found!" Pooh waved the bullhorn in the air. Then he slipped through the fence and walked toward the pawing, snorting animal.

Just then Piglet and Tigger arrived. "Pooh! Be careful!" yelled Piglet.

"Oh, hello there, Piglet," Pooh shouted back. He turned his back on the bull and walked toward Piglet.

Seeing Pooh in his pen, the bull began to get angry. His snorts grew louder, and his pawing became wilder.

"Oh, d-dear!" gasped Piglet. "The bull is going to charge. I've got to do something!" Piglet ran to the nearby picnic area, snatched a red tablecloth from one of the tables, and leapt into the bullpen. At that very moment the bull began to charge right at Pooh.

Brave Piglet waved the red tablecloth in the air. The bull saw it and stopped charging at Pooh. "Hurray!" shouted Piglet. "Oh, dear! Perhaps my 'Hurray' was a bit early. Now it looks like the bull is charging at me!" Piglet turned and ran. The charging bull was gaining on Piglet with each step.

"Hold tight, little buddy!" shouted Tigger as he jumped into the pen. "One dramatic-type rescue coming right up!" Just as the bull was about to reach Piglet, Tigger scooped up his little friend and bounced a huge bounce up to the safety of an overhanging tree.

"Wow, Tigger!" said Piglet. "Can you teach me to
bounce like that?"
"Not now, kiddo," replied Tigger. "What about Pooh?"

Back in the pen Pooh turned once more and started to bring the bullhorn over to the bull. Again the beast grunted and snorted and pawed the ground, then began to charge at Pooh.

But walking toward the bull, Pooh tripped over a rock and fell. As Pooh hit the ground, his nose pressed the button that turned on the bullhorn. "Oh, bother," said Pooh, lying facedown in the grass. The bullhorn made his voice sound very loud, and it boomed across the pen.

The loud noise startled the bull, who stopped his charge and curiously looked at Pooh. The bull had never heard a bear make this kind of sound before.

Pooh picked himself up and walked over to the bull. "I believe this is yours," he said as he tied the horn onto the bull's head.

When the puzzled bull grunted, Pooh simply replied, "Why, you're welcome, my friend. I'm sure you would do the same for me—if I had lost a horn, that is!"

Pooh said good-bye to the bull, left the pen, and rejoined his friends. "Way to go, Buddy Bear," said Tigger. "I couldn't have done better myself!"

"That was a very brave thing you did, Pooh!" said Piglet.

"Not at all, Piglet," replied Pooh. "I was just being polite. Now, you are both invited to my house. Breakfast is long overdue!"